The Amazing Adventures of
Teddy Tum Tum

First U. S. Edition 1992

ISBN 1-55970-185-4
Library of Congress Catalog Card Number 91-73948
Library of Congress Cataloging-in-Publication information is available.

Published in the United States by Arcade Publishing, Inc., New York,
a Little, Brown company, by arrangement with Michael O'Mara Books Ltd.

1 3 5 7 9 10 8 6 4 2

Printed in Belgium

The Amazing Adventures of
Teddy Tum Tum

Illustrated by Patrick Lowry
Written by Gillian Breese and Tony Langham

Arcade Publishing • New York

LITTLE, BROWN AND COMPANY

It was just after naptime in the playroom. All the toys were sitting around, listening to the rain pitter-patter on the windowpane. Teddy Tum Tum didn't like rain because it meant staying indoors. He wanted to be outside on one of his adventures.

"Never mind," said Rose-Anne the Rag Doll. "Why don't you tell us about one of your adventures instead?"

"Great idea!" said Putney. "Tell them about the time we were captured by the Bongo Bongo tribe."

"Oh, all right," agreed Teddy Tum Tum.

The toys gathered around to listen.

"It was a very dangerous mission," Tum Tum told them. "We had to make careful plans for the perilous journey."

"Where were you going?" asked one of the toys, already beginning to feel frightened.

"Into the unknown, up the Great River Rambardo, where no bear had ever been before. It was full of wild animals with huge eyes.

"I couldn't go alone. Too dangerous. So I took my trusty friend Putney Bear to carry supplies."

"Did you take a map?" asked another toy.

"Adventurers don't use maps!" scoffed Tum Tum. "We used our eyes and our ears and set sail into the unknown."

"There was danger everywhere. Great big slimy creatures with rocks on their backs, huge hairy eight-legged beasts, watching and waiting, waiting and watching. Would they pounce, would they attack? We had no way of knowing. But there was no turning back. We paddled on deeper and deeper into the unknown and then . . . disaster struck."

Rose-Anne gasped.

"The Great River Rambardo flowed faster and faster. The water swirled around us, waves crashed onto the deck. We tried to steer the boat through the raging torrent. It began to fill with water. Bailing didn't do any good.

"All our supplies were thrown into the muddy water. Poor Putney was washed overboard. I barely managed to grab his ear as he floated past me. Then the boat started to sink. We scrambled to the bank, exhausted, and collapsed, glad we were still alive."

"Our boat was wrecked. Our supplies were lost. Our stuffing was all wet. But Putney and I didn't give up. We rested for a while and talked about what to do. There was only one thing to do — continue on foot."

"We headed off into the jungle not knowing what danger lay ahead."

"Were you scared?" asked Sammy the Soldier.

"Not really," answered Tum Tum. "I'd been in situations more dangerous than this before."

"Go on," begged Sammy. "Please!"

"I led the way and Putney followed right behind. Every step led us closer to danger. Now it was getting dark, and shadows rose menacingly in front of us, but we crept forward cautiously, a step at a time, looking and listening, listening and looking."

"Putney thought he saw things."

"What things?" asked Eric the Elephant, not really wanting to know the answer.

"Hard to say. Just *things*."

Rose-Anne covered her face, barely able to listen.

"We could feel eyes watching us, following us. We couldn't see them, but we knew they were there. We marched on and on. Then we saw *it*."

"We came face to face with the monster. It was huge. It was horrible. It sat there looking down at us with blazing yellow eyes."

"What did you do?" gasped Eric.

"Under the circumstances and all things considered, I gave the order to retreat."

"What does that mean?" asked Rose-Anne.

"Run away," said Putney.

"Retreat means retreat!" huffed Tum Tum. "Now, can I go on?"

"We ran through the undergrowth. Sharp prickers clawed at our fur. Suddenly I was stopped dead in my tracks by a sharp pain in my ear. It had caught on a long spiky thorn and I was stuck. As I tried to free myself, I could hear the monster gaining on me.

"I pulled with all my might, ripping my ear free just in time. We ran and ran until we could run no more. We dared to stop a moment to see if the monster was still following us. We turned around but only saw the bushes moving where we had forced our way through."

"We wandered in this strange land for days until we finally came to a clearing in the jungle. In the middle of the clearing stood a tall stone with a huge dial on top.

"What was it? It was so tall that the dial cast a great shadow over us."

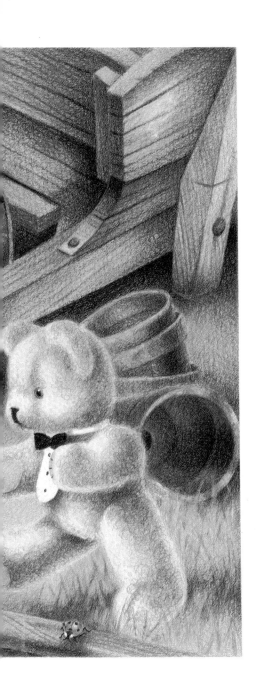

"As we explored the clearing we found some puzzling objects, like a long spear with twelve sharp prongs and a wagon with only one wheel.

"Suddenly I felt myself falling. Putney tried to save me, but it was no use. I'd fallen into a bear trap!

"In a matter of seconds we were surrounded by the fiercest hunters in the land, the Bongo Bongo tribe from Argar Don."

"Someone grabbed me and threw me into the wagon. Poor Putney was dumped beside me and then the wagon began to move. Where were we going and why?

"We seemed to go around and around, but at last we came to a halt. Was this the end? Would we ever see our friends again?"

"We ended up in the clearing, next to the stone tower. We were lifted out and put right on top of it.

"I told Putney to be brave and prepare for the worst. There was a piercing cry from one of the tribe and then they surrounded us, dancing and hollering.

"The dance ended as suddenly as it started. The Bongo Bongo tribe became suddenly silent and still. Then they walked toward us. We closed our eyes."

"Go on, go on," pleaded Rose-Anne.

"It turned out they didn't want to hurt us at all. As a matter of fact, they wanted to be our friends. And guess what they did?"

"What?" said Rose-Anne, her eyes big as saucers.

"They made us members of their tribe! They put golden crowns covered with fabulous jewels on our heads."

"Wow!" exclaimed Eric.

"Yes, it was pretty exciting, but that's just *one* of the adventures I've had."

"Really?" said Rose-Anne, her eyes wide with wonder. "Please tell us more."

Teddy Tum Tum smiled to himself.
"More later," he replied. "And be-
sides," he said, "it's stopped raining. Look,
the sun's coming out!"